ISSUNBŌSHI

ISSUNBŌSHI

ILLUSTRATED BY

George Suyeoka

ADAPTED FROM THE ORIGINAL FOLKTALES BY

Robert B. Goodman
and Robert A. Spicer

ISLAND HERITAGE

EDITORS
Robert B. Goodman
Robert A. Spicer

ASSOCIATE EDITOR
Carol A. Jenkins

CONSULTING EDITORS
Ruth Tabrah
Rubellite K. Johnson
Frances Kakugawa
George A. Fargo
Jodi Belknap
Kirsten Whatley

Published and distributed by

94-411 KŌʻAKI STREET • WAIPAHU, HAWAIʻI 96797
ORDERS: (800) 468-2800 • INFORMATION: (808) 564-8800
FAX: (808) 564-8877 • **islandheritage.com**

ISBN: 0-89610-042-1
2ND EDITION, 1ST PRINTING - 2003

IN THE PROVINCE OF SETTSU, in a village that is now Osaka, there once lived a couple who dreamed of a child of their own.

Year after year they climbed to the temple to ask the gods for a son.

The wife, Yaye, wanted a child so badly that one day she cried out: "I would be happy, o gods, for a boy-child even if he were no bigger than my thumb!"

3

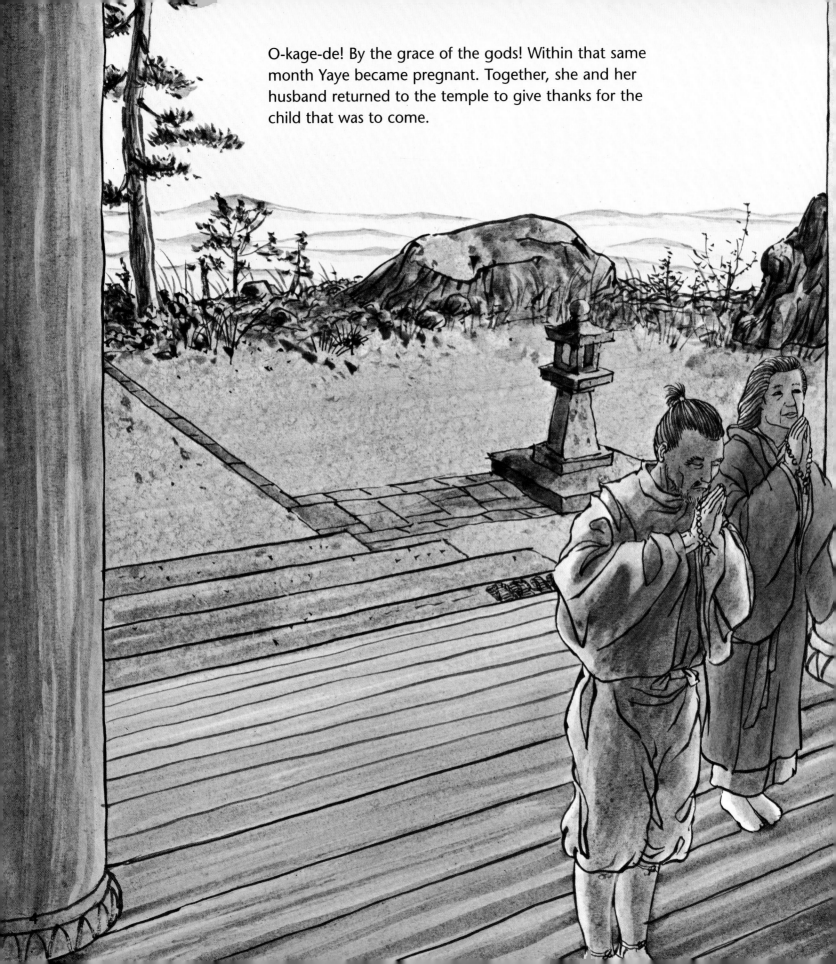

O-kage-de! By the grace of the gods! Within that same month Yaye became pregnant. Together, she and her husband returned to the temple to give thanks for the child that was to come.

The day of the birth was joy—and astonishment!
"Yaye, the gods listened well to you, woman! He is no bigger
than your thumb, indeed!

"Issunbōshi! One-inch boy. That is the name I give our son."

6

With loving patience they waited for the boy
to grow bigger. He did not.

One grain of rice, a drop of tea, the tiniest
fish was a feast for Issunbōshi.

Children came from all over the village to see him. They loved to play hide-and-seek and Issunbōshi, always smiling and happy, always won.

He could hide anywhere. The children learned quickly to take care not to step on the little fellow. Everybody loved him.

"Oto-sama," said Issunbōshi, pointing up the river towards Kyoto, the city of the Emperor. "I will soon be sixteen. It is time for me to go out into the world. Give me permission to leave, Father. I would like to serve in the house of a great lord."

His father nodded. "Our house will be lonely without you, my son. But it is true, you are sixteen. It is time to find your place as a man!

"Come, Yaye, we must prepare our son for his journey."

There was much to do—food, weapons, clothing, and a boat were needed. A sewing needle became a sharp sword, hari-no-ken.

A soup bowl, owan, made a splendid boat, and hashi, a chopstick, was the oar.

His mother made a dumpling bag—mochi no fukuro—and filled it with food. She knew her son would be hungry on his journey.

"Make your fortune in the world with honor to the Emperor and to us," said the old man as he launched his son into the stream.

"Remember, your grandfather was once a vice minister."

Yaye wiped away a mother's tears. "Genki-de! Be careful!" she called. "Sayonara!"

Keeping to the shallows, where the current eddied, Issunbōshi began the long and difficult river journey. The smallest waves threatened to upset the owan-no-fune.

He learned to scull with the hashi, working it in a churning motion to propel the boat along.

A sudden rain shower filled him with panic. "The rain will fill my boat and I'll drown!" He sculled with all his might to get into the shelter of a lily pad.

The shower passed.

Issunbōshi was just casting off when a giant frog, in search of insects, landed beside him with a great splash. The frog fixed his two great yellow eyes on the tiny warrior and prepared to swallow him.

Quick as a flash, Issunbōshi parried the darting tongue. The surprised frog stopped for a moment, then renewed his attack.

The boy fought with all his strength but he was no match for the giant frog.

The deadly tongue lashed out again and Issunbōshi felt himself being lifted into the air. He was certain that he would soon be inside the frog's gaping mouth.

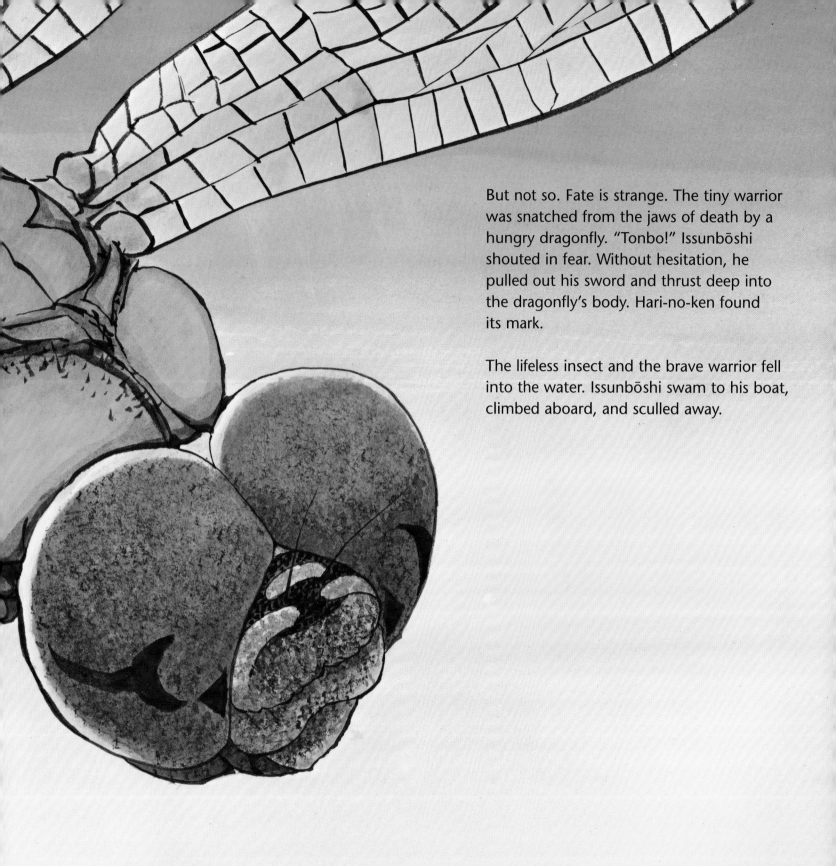

But not so. Fate is strange. The tiny warrior was snatched from the jaws of death by a hungry dragonfly. "Tonbo!" Issunbōshi shouted in fear. Without hesitation, he pulled out his sword and thrust deep into the dragonfly's body. Hari-no-ken found its mark.

The lifeless insect and the brave warrior fell into the water. Issunbōshi swam to his boat, climbed aboard, and sculled away.

Weary, sore, and hungry after many days, Issunbōshi sighted the temples and castle walls of the city of Kyoto.

No one noticed the tiny owan-no-fune on the busy surface of the river.

Issunbōshi found a landing place between two rocks. With hari-no-ken sheathed at his side, he clambered ashore.

26

Such traffic! Issunbōshi dodged for his life.
How to find the house of a great lord in all
this confusion?

I must! Issunbōshi resolved. I will pledge
my sword for a great lord's defense and
honor. Then I can prove I'm a man and a
brave fighter!

I will try this one! thought Issunbōshi as he finally stood before the gate of the biggest house in the city.

He dusted his clothing, wiped the dirt from his face, and stood proudly his full inch.

Late evening shadows were gathering as his tiny bell-like voice called out, "Your Lordship! I am Issunbōshi! I have come to offer my services! Open your gate!"

Now it so happened that the Lord of the House was the Emperor's Prime Minister, a very sensitive man. Evening would find him in the garden listening to the insect symphony. Cicadas singing at sunset. Bees humming drowsily off for the night. This was the music that soothed him at the end of the day.

What strange sound is that? he wondered when he heard Issunbōshi calling.

He spoke to his attendant. "Open the gate carefully! I must see what that is!"

"I am Issunbōshi" cried the young warrior. "I have come to serve you. I am the grandson of Horikawa!"

"Ah, so?" smiled the Prime Minister. "That is a famous name, Horikawa-Sama. And that is a fine sword you have, Issunbōshi. I like the sound of you! I accept you into my service.

"Miyuki!" The Prime Minister called for his daughter. "Here is your new bodyguard."

And so it was that Issunbōshi became a court favorite.
His friendly manner, his warm smile, and his fierce defense
of Miyuki won everyone's love and respect.
He accompanied her everywhere.

The Princess preferred Issunbōshi above all others. Affection grew between them as the seasons yielded—spring to summer, summer to the enchantment of the harvest moon.

For Issunbōshi it was also a difficult time. He was first a warrior pledged to protect her, yet his heart ached with love for the beautiful Miyuki. But how could he speak of love when he was hardly bigger than her thumb?

"Issunbōshi!" Miyuki's young voice called out one morning. "We must get ready. Today we must go to the Shrine at Ise."

For the first time the tiny warrior did not want to go along. He knew that this was the journey every young maiden must take. At the shrine, Miyuki would pray for a husband, a full-sized man.

Hiding his tears, Issunbōshi led the Princess safely on the long journey to Ise.

But as Miyuki left the temple, two evil oni attacked without warning. Only Issunbōshi whirled to face the monsters. The other attendants fled in terror.

"Who are you?" laughed the oni. "A needle for a sword? Ha! I'll crush you with my little finger."

43

Issunbōshi seized his chance. "Ei!" he shouted.

His needle-sharp sword plunged deep into the monster's eye.

Blinded, and bellowing with pain, the monster dropped Issunbōshi and ran away.

45

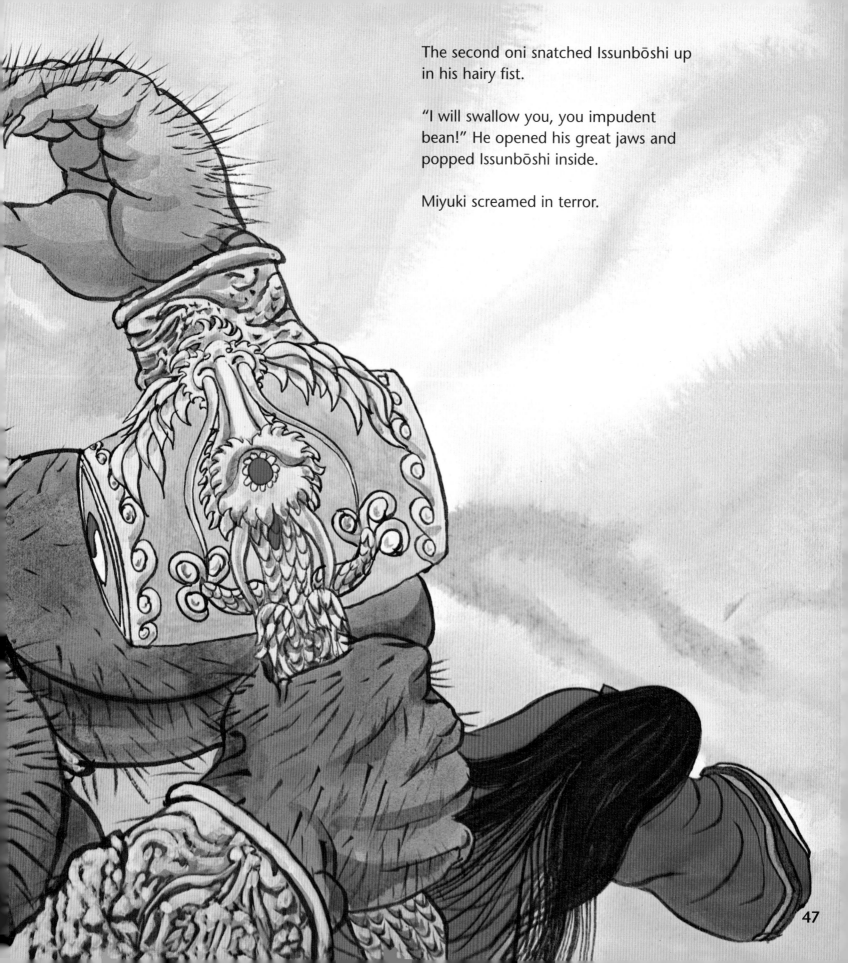

The second oni snatched Issunbōshi up in his hairy fist.

"I will swallow you, you impudent bean!" He opened his great jaws and popped Issunbōshi inside.

Miyuki screamed in terror.

Inside the monster's mouth, the tiny
warrior dodged the great teeth. Bracing
himself, he buried hari-no-ken deep into
the monster's throat.

The oni coughed with a painful roar. Issunbōshi was hurled out of the monster's mouth and landed in the soft black hair of his beloved Miyuki.

Miyuki was overjoyed. Tenderly, she held Issunbōshi.

"I thought I would never see you again. I was so afraid and you were so brave!" Issunbōshi swelled with pride. He had proved his courage as a warrior.

52

"Look, Issunbōshi! The monsters dropped their magic mallet! If we strike it," said Miyuki eagerly, "we can have any wish our hearts desire!

"Make a wish, my brave warrior!"

For Issunbōshi, there was only one wish—to be a full-sized man.

The mallet shimmered with a blinding golden light. When they could see again—the Issunbōshi who was no bigger than his father's thumb had disappeared. In his place stood a handsome young man.

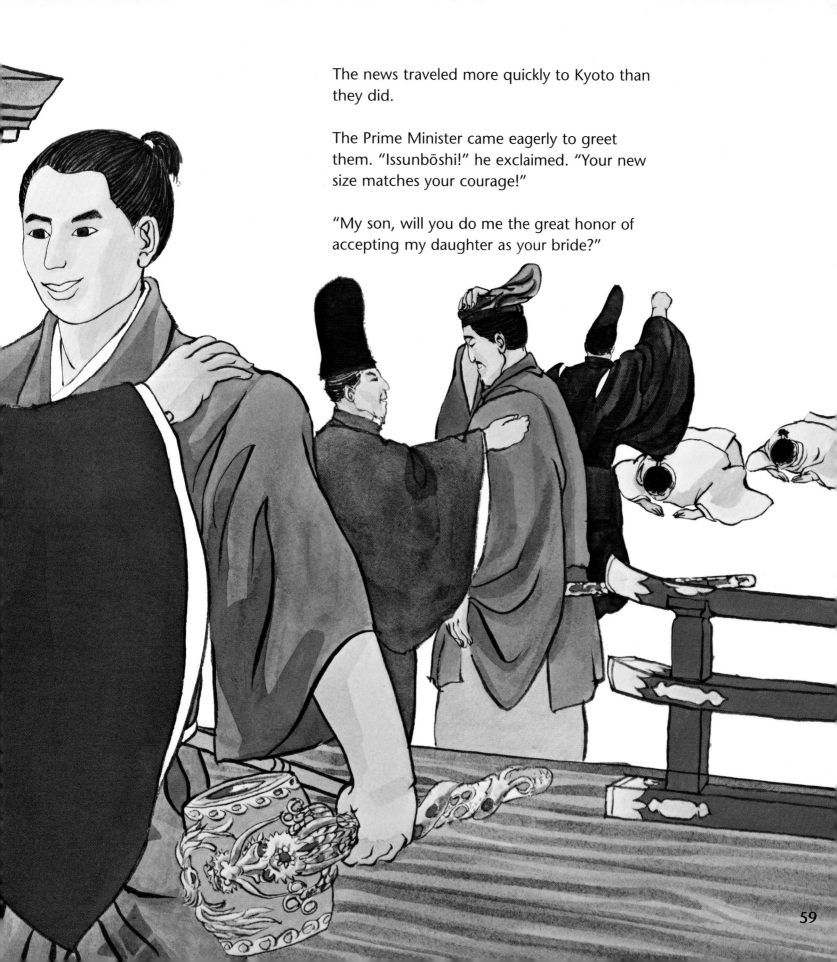

The news traveled more quickly to Kyoto than they did.

The Prime Minister came eagerly to greet them. "Issunbōshi!" he exclaimed. "Your new size matches your courage!"

"My son, will you do me the great honor of accepting my daughter as your bride?"

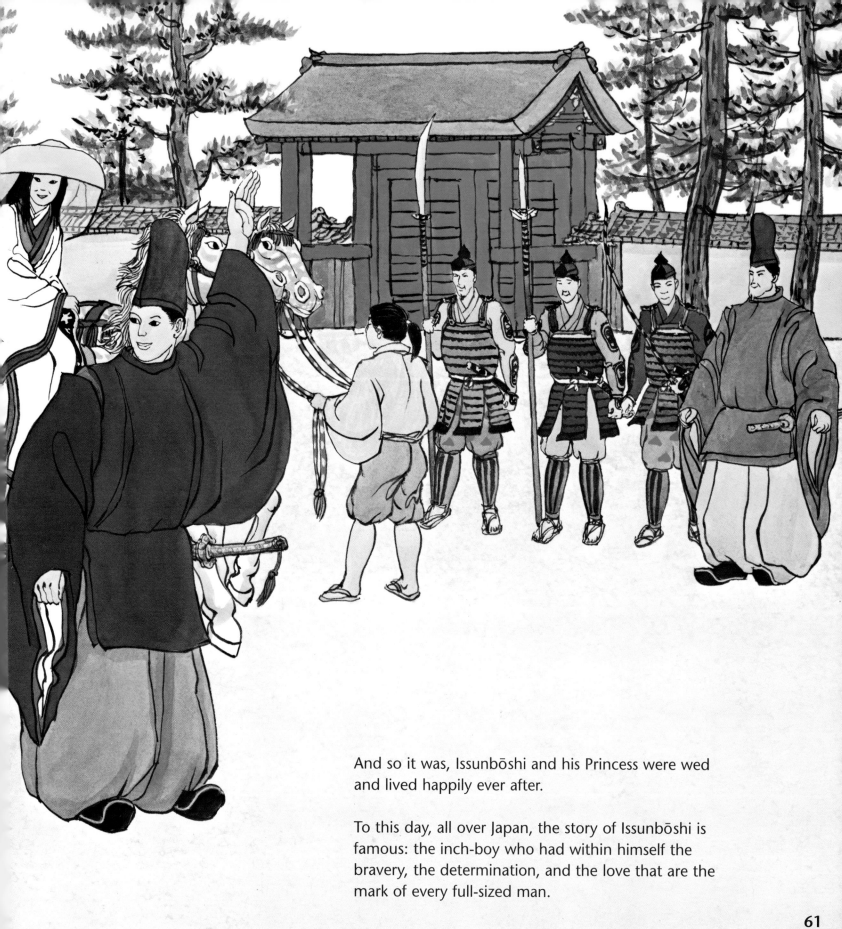

And so it was, Issunbōshi and his Princess were wed and lived happily ever after.

To this day, all over Japan, the story of Issunbōshi is famous: the inch-boy who had within himself the bravery, the determination, and the love that are the mark of every full-sized man.

An Introduction to Things Japanese

The Japanese objects shown here are generally vintage Heian to Muromachi (700 A.D. to 1200 A.D.)

A. Red lacquered soup bowl (*owan*)
B. Iron sewing needle
C. Bamboo chopstick (*hashi*)

A

B

C

D. Cart or carriage, ox drawn
E. Straw slippers
F. Aristocratic shoes of leather and silk
G. Lacquered clogs
H. Kannon Bosatsu: Goddess of mercy and benevolence

D

E   F   G   H

62

L. Oni, demon, carrying his gold and jewel-encrusted jade magic hammer

I. Wood lacquer inlay saddle and gilt inlay stirrups (metal)

J. & K. Aristocratic hats (now primarily the symbol of the emperor's head-gear and of Shinto priests)

I

J

K

L

English version for the music by Judy and Masato Sato.

Ky -ō e ha -ru -ba -ru no bo - ri yu -ku
He sets out for Kyoto's shore where he's sure fortune lies.

2. Kyō wa Sanjō no daijin-dono ni
   Kakaeraretaru Issunbōshi
   Hōshi, Hōshi to okini-iri
   Hime no otomo de kiyomizu e

3. Satemo kaeri no Kiyomizu-zaka ni
   Oni ga ippiki araware idete
   Kutte kakareba sono kuchi e
   Hōshi tachimachi odorikomu

4. Hari no tachi oba sakate ni motte
   Chikuri, chikuri to harajū tsukeba
   Oni was Hōshi o hakidashite
   Isshōkenmei ni nigete yuku

5. Oni ga wasureta Uchide no Kozuchi
   Uteba fushigi ya Issunbōshi
   Hito uchi goto ni sei ga nobite
   Ima was rippana ō - otoko

2. Long and hard was his trip to Kyoto City,
   "At your service, my lord, I am Issunbōshi,"
   cried the small warrior at the great lord's gate.
   "I will surely serve you well!" said Issunbōshi.

3. Off they go to the temple on the mountain
   Princess, daughter of the lord, and Issunbōshi
   From the shadows there sprang an oni fierce,
   Issunbōshi jumped into his mouth

4. Hari no tachi was his trusty blade.
   Stabbing, jabbing in the oni's throat did he fight, and then
   Screeching, yelling, the oni spit him out,
   Running, howling, the oni ran from him.

5. Left behind on the ground, a magic mallet.
   "Hurry, hurry, make your wish now, Issunbōshi!"
   Came a blinding flash and when it was gone,
   Issunbōshi was a full-grown man.

Fukaku Kansha-shimafu

Island Heritage is grateful to
Fumiyo Anematsu, Dr. Hiroko Ikeda,
Keiko Takeuchi, and Judy and Masato
Sato for their contributions to Issunbōshi.

We also wish to thank Edward R. Bendet,
and Martin I. Rosenberg. Special
thanks go to Mr. and Mrs. Paul Slavey,
Ron Gandee, Robert Lee, Penny McCracken
and Elizabeth Owen of Pacific Phototype, Inc.